First American Edition 2016
Kane Miller, A Division of EDC Publishing

Cover design and illustrations by Dyani Stagg of Merchantwise
Text, design and illustrations copyright © Lemonfizz Media 2011
First published by Scholastic Australia Pty Limited in 2011
This edition published under license from Scholastic Australia Pty
Limited on behalf of Lemonfizz Media

For information contact:
Kane Miller, A Division of EDC Publishing
P.O. Box 470663
Tulsa, OK 74147-0663
www.kanemiller.com
www.edcpub.com
www.usbornebooksandmore.com

Library of Congress Control Number: 2015953931

Printed and bound in the United States of America
1 2 3 4 5 6 7 8 9 10

ISBN: 978-1-61067-509-3

# DRAMA QUEEN

## SUSANNAH MCFARLANE

A DIVISION OF EDC PUBLISHING

Sydney Radisson's cat was named
by Emma Chapman

# Chapter • 1

It was late Saturday afternoon. Emma threw her gymnastics bag in the hall closet and raced to her room. She had performed her best beam routine ever and she wanted to write about it in her diary before she forgot how she felt. She went straight to the secret spot under her beanbag and reached underneath. There was nothing there. Emma scrunched her nose and frowned as she picked the beanbag right up off the floor and shook it hard. The diary had to be there; she'd put it back carefully that morning, she was sure of it. But it wasn't.

Perhaps she'd forgotten to put it back in its

usual place? Emma looked on her desk and under her bed. But there was still no diary. *What had happened to it or,* she suddenly thought, *what had someone* done *to it? Had someone found it and taken it?* Emma's mind raced. *Who has taken my diary?* This needed investigating, now. She stomped out of her room.

"Someone has taken my diary," she yelled to no one in particular, now convinced that this was what had happened. No one answered.

She continued stomping down the hallway and stopped outside her brother Bob's bedroom. Emma looked in through the open door and there, in the middle of the floor, on a pile of disgustingly dirty clothes, was her diary. Open.

"No!" cried Emma, horrified, but, as she went to pick up the diary, she saw that it was even worse. There were muddy, smudgy marks all over the page and one of the corners was torn. "It's ruined!" Emma gasped. "Did Bob do this?"

Emma, her face nearly scarlet with anger, raced

into the kitchen where Bob, still in his dirty soccer gear, was drinking a glass of milk. Dad was stirring the pasta and Mom was reading the newspaper. Emma looked from Bob in his muddy soccer clothes to the dirty pages of her diary, found in his room. She was right; it was Bob who'd taken it.

Emma exploded. "Look at this!" she shouted. Mom, Dad and Bob spun around, looking slightly alarmed. "It's ruined, completely ruined. I won't be able to use it ever again! And," she added, yelling and looking straight at Bob, "it's all *your* fault!"

"What?" said Bob, his mouth hanging open. "What is?"

"Don't pretend you don't know what I'm talking about!" cried Emma.

"I don't need to pretend, I *don't* have any idea what you are talking about," replied Bob. "Mom, Dad, I promise I don't."

"You, you, you—*brother!*" Emma spluttered in fury. "You've ruined my diary!"

"I didn't even know you had a diary," said Bob.

"You did so! And you found my secret hiding spot and now you've ruined it with your dirty soccer cleats or your dirty hands or your, your dirty something. It's not fair, why do you have to be so mean?" Emma's eyes were watering and she was angry, so angry that she didn't notice that Bob was looking blankly at her, completely confused. She kept going. "And you read it and you put your stupid muddy soccer mud all over it! And then you …"

"I did not," said Bob flatly. "And, anyway, when would I have done it? I've been at soccer all afternoon."

Emma ignored him and turned to her parents. "Mom! Dad! Say something!"

"I was hoping you might calm down a bit first," said Dad.

"How can I be calm? My stupid brother has ruined my diary!"

"Are you sure Bob took it?" he said, peering over at the diary. Continuing in an irritatingly calm voice, he added, "Are you sure it is ruined? It looks like

10

only a few little spots and I reckon we could—"

Emma broke in, not giving him a chance to finish.

"They're *not* little spots, they're *huge* dirty spots and they are right across the page, probably the most important page in the whole book!" cried Emma. "It *is* ruined, completely ruined!"

"Get a grip, Emma. You're such a drama queen!" said Bob.

"I am not!" Emma screeched rather dramatically.

"You so are!" replied Bob. "I didn't touch your diary. Why would I want to?"

"Because, because …" Emma couldn't actually think of a good reason, but it didn't stop her being convinced that it was Bob's fault. "Because you're a mean brother! Because you did!"

"I didn't," repeated Bob. "Drama queen!"

"Dad!" cried Emma.

"Well, you might be overreacting just a little," suggested Dad.

"Mom!" Emma looked to her mother pleadingly.

"I'm *not* being a drama queen, am I?"

But her mother just smiled. Emma knew what that smile meant. Her mother agreed with the others. She did think Emma was overreacting.

"Gee whizz, lemonfizz!" cried Emma. "I'm *not* being unreasonable!"

And with that, Emma stomped unreasonably out of the kitchen, back up the hall and into her bedroom, slamming the door hard behind her. She heard the plaque with her name on it fall onto the floor and break. Now even grumpier, she threw herself down onto her beanbag and folded her arms tightly across her chest. "Why doesn't *anyone* understand?" she fumed to herself. "I'm *not* being unreasonable. It is my special, secret diary and now it is not special anymore. Who wouldn't get angry about that?"

But somewhere quite deep down, just for a moment, Emma thought that maybe she might have gotten a little carried away. Still, Bob shouldn't have taken her diary. Now that she thought about it, how did Bob find it? It had been so well hidden. No one could have suspected anything was under her beanbag—could they? Then the thought that she may have hidden it badly crossed her mind. Emma felt worse. After all, what sort of secret agent must she be if she couldn't even hide a diary from her brother?

Being a secret agent, that was Emma Jacks' other secret thing. When she wasn't a schoolgirl, a gymnast and an irritated sister of Bob Jacks, she was Special Agent EJ12, field agent and code-cracker in the under-twelve division of the **SHINE** agency.

**SHINE** was an international agency that helped keep the world safe from the plots of evildoers, particularly those belonging to the *SHADOW* agency, which was as bad as **SHINE** was good. *SHADOW* was constantly launching new schemes that endangered the environment and the world;

SHINE was constantly sending its agents out to find and stop *SHADOW*. SHINE had agents of all ages, all with special talents that they could use to help in the fight against *SHADOW*. But a secret agency couldn't simply put an advertisement in the paper or on the Internet for special agents. Instead, they had quieter ways to find clever, good people to work for them. They had found Emma Jacks at an inter-school math competition.

Emma loved math; she loved the way it always made sense and didn't change, that the answer was always the same answer and you could always find that answer if you found the right clues. And that was why SHINE wanted Emma: they needed code-crackers, people who looked calmly at a problem, patiently found the clues and cracked the code. They then used that decoded message to stop the evil scheme. And as EJ12, Emma was a great agent, in fact one of SHINE's best. She always stayed calm and thought things through.

But Emma Jacks was not doing any of that now.

As she sat on her beanbag furiously writing in her dirty diary, she didn't think anything of her kitten, Inky, walking off with her hair ribbon. It just made her more annoyed.

"Oh great," she cried. "Now everyone is taking my stuff!"

And she certainly didn't notice Inky's dirty paws as the kitten walked out of her bedroom and padded her muddy way down the hallway.

# Chapter · 2

Later that evening, after a sulky dinner, things were calmer. Dad and Bob had gone out to a movie and it was just Emma and her mom at home, stretched out on the sofa together in front of the TV. Well, just Emma and Mom if you didn't count the animals, which Emma always did. Emma was lying on the couch with her head on a cushion on her mom's lap. Pip, their husky puppy, was tucked in behind her and Inky was sitting against her tummy, purring. So it was just the four girls. Emma liked that; no irritating, diary-dirtying brother and she had her mom all to herself. Her mom was playing with

Emma's hair while Emma munched on the warm popcorn they had just made together. Pip, who was looking intently at the bowl, seemed to be thinking she might like to eat some popcorn, but Emma didn't agree.

*This is nice,* Emma thought to herself. *The movie is about to begin and I still haven't gotten in trouble for all that yelling.*

"Em," her mom began.

*Uh-oh, here it comes,* Emma thought. She knew from the tone of her mom's voice that "a talk" was about to begin. Emma didn't really want to have "a talk." She wanted to eat popcorn and watch the movie while her mom stroked her hair. And, anyway, the whole thing was over now. She was sorry she had yelled at Bob. Well she wasn't actually, but she *was* sorry she had yelled at her mom and dad. Was that a good start? She thought she would try it out.

"I'm sorry I yelled, Mom," said Emma, looking up at her mom with what was, she hoped, her most endearing expression.

"Thank you, Em," said her mom.

Emma was rather hoping that would be the end of it, but she doubted it.

"You did make rather a fuss …"

"But my diary …" Emma began.

"That's no excuse," replied Mom. "You really went over the top, shouting at everyone. The diary isn't ruined and you don't even know it was Bob who got it dirty."

"Well, who else would it be?" muttered Emma sulkily.

"I don't know, but things are not always how they seem. I also don't see how Bob could have done it if it happened before soccer, but he only got dirty after soccer."

*Hmmm,* thought Emma. That was a good point. No wonder her mom had been such a good **SHINE** agent. Her mom's code name was SJ45R. The R stood for "retired": with her family and her work, Emma's mom didn't really have time for missions anymore. She did, however, have time to be backup for Emma, EJ12, if she needed it on missions. Mom was part of EJ12's BEST network. **SHINE** knew that agents often needed support, so they created the BEST agent assistance system. BEST stood for Brains, Expertise, Support and Tips and each agent had their own, security-cleared network of BESTies, as they were called, who could help them on missions. "Don't get depressed, call a best!" was one of **SHINE**'s many mottos. The BEST system was great, but there was one rule—an agent could never discuss her spy work outside a mission. It was much too risky; you never knew who might be listening. Em might not be able to talk about her work, but it was still good to know her mom understood. She snuggled into her, hoping their talk was over.

"So, Em," continued Mom, "don't sweat the small stuff, don't get upset about things that don't matter and ..."

"Yes?" asked Emma.

"You will need to apologize to Bob."

"But …"

"No, no buts. You need to apologize to Bob in the morning."

"Mom!"

"No, Emma. It is too silly to get so worked up about little things. You can do better than that," said Mom. "Okay, that's the lecture over." Emma's mom smiled down at her daughter. "Pass the popcorn. The movie is about to start."

They both looked at the TV screen as the studio logo came up. Then the screen went black before large white letters appeared, as if they were being keyed onto a computer screen.

SPY MOVIE

"They won't know anything about what real secret agents do," said Mom. "It should be a hoot!"

And then, a long-legged woman with impossibly straight and impossibly blond hair, dressed in a black trench coat and wearing dark glasses appeared on the screen. As she peered over the glasses, revealing very long and definitely not real eyelashes, the shot froze as the screen split in half, with one half going black again as more letters appeared.

SYDNEY RADISSON
IS AGENT WHITE

"Now *there's* a real drama queen," said Mom. Sydney Radisson was a young actor who did seem to be known more for her tantrums on set than her acting skills. She played the main secret agent in the film. "She doesn't even look like a real spy! As if she could do a mission in those heels!"

"And Agent White!" laughed Emma. "What sort of a code name is that?"

"Ridiculous," agreed Mom. "And look at her nails! Okay, it's starting. Let's see how many mistakes we can find."

And Emma and her mom spent the whole film finding spy errors, eating popcorn and giggling. Emma still wasn't convinced Bob hadn't ruined her diary, but she had stopped worrying about it.

Which was just as well because *SHADOW* was acting up again and **SHINE** was going to need clearheaded agents who could see the big picture. Correction, they were going to need a clearheaded EJ12.

# Chapter · 3

The next morning, the radio was on in the kitchen as Bob and Emma were getting themselves breakfast. Emma tipped some granola into a bowl and was about to put the container back in the cupboard when she looked across to Bob who had, as usual, his head in the fridge. She smiled to herself and opened the drawer with the pots and pans instead. As she did, Bob turned around and saw her.

"Hey, I want that," said Bob.

"Oh, sorry," said Emma, "I was just putting it away."

"In the pots and pans drawer?"

"Oh, it's just a new secret place—you should have no problems finding that, should you?" said Emma, smiling a little too sweetly.

"Emma, get over it!" exclaimed Bob. "I did *not* take your stupid diary and I have no idea how the pages got so dirty."

Emma banged and clanged a lot of saucepans and felt her face growing hot as she started to get irritated all over again.

"Hey, what's all this noise?" cried Mom, as she walked into the kitchen. "Emma, I thought you had something to say to Bob?"

Emma clanged a pan and glared at Bob as she whispered, "Thanks, now you've gotten me in trouble again!"

"Come on, you two," said Mom. "Sit down and eat your breakfast. Bob, can you turn up the radio, please? It's time for the news."

Dad came into the kitchen and sat down at the table. As the family ate their breakfast, they all listened to the news bulletin.

"In breaking news this morning, there has been a disturbing discovery at one of the city's reservoirs. Staff were stunned to discover that the water had turned into pink gel-like balls. Police are on-site, but have so far found no explanation for what has happened and experts are being rushed to the scene. We will keep you up-to-date as this story develops."

Emma stopped eating and looked at her mom. No explanation: that was unusual.

"Movie star Sydney Radisson flew into town last night," the newsreader continued. "She has jetted in to film her final location scenes of *Spy Movie 2—Black and White*, the long-awaited sequel to last summer's popular comedy, *Spy Movie.* The film is being shot on location for the next month and although details are top secret, insiders have leaked that this movie will be set around water. And now to the weather …"

"That's funny," chuckled Bob. "Get it? Leaked, about water, water leaking!"

"Very funny, Bob," said Dad, laughing as he tied his running shoes and headed for the door. "I'm off for my run, keep up the jokes, Bob."

But Emma and Mom weren't in a joking mood. Mom turned off the radio and looked at Emma. Emma opened her mouth to speak but was interrupted—

Piinngg!

It was Emma's phone, which was no ordinary phone. It was a **SHINE** special-issue phone. It looked like a cross between a gaming console and a touch screen phone. If you swiped the screen in a particular way, a new screen would appear with special **SHINE** apps: code-cracking apps, invisible ink-reading apps, animal files, fingerprint-testing apps and more. The phone also had special ringtones and the one that had just sounded was a mission alert, telling the agent to report to **SHINE HQ** immediately. Emma looked at her mom, Mom looked at Emma, then they both looked at Bob, who was still eating his way through an enormous bowl of granola. He wouldn't notice a thing.

Emma took her phone from her pocket and looked at the screen. The alert was flashing.

REPORT HQ FOR MISSION.
ACCESS VIA LIGHT SHOP.

"Oh, Mom, I've forgotten," said Emma, trying to make her voice sound light and casual. "I was going over to Isi's place today. I'm supposed to be there now. Will you drive me?"

Emma's mom smiled. "Oh, yes, so you are, Em! We'd better get going."

"That's great, thanks. I'll just get a few things from my room."

Emma got up, put her bowl in the dishwasher and ran to her room, shutting the door behind her.

She went to her desk and opened the second-from-the-top desk drawer. She then felt under the right-hand side of the desk and pressed a small button that dropped down when the drawer opened. Immediately, a book in her bookshelf popped out onto the floor. Emma picked it up and opened the cover to reveal a small safe with a keypad. Emma keyed in 3-8-1-20-13 and opened the safe.

Inside was a charm bracelet, but, just like her phone, this was no ordinary charm bracelet. It was a **SHINE**-issue CHARM bracelet, with the letters standing for Clever Hidden Accessories with Release Mechanism. Each little charm on the bracelet was actually a spy gadget. A simple twist of the charm and it would convert to a piece of spy equipment. There were charms for listening devices, charms to repel dangerous animals, charms to attract animals, charms to help you climb, charms to help you see in the dark—there seemed to be a **SHINE** charm for everything and more were always being invented. Who would ever suspect that a simple charm bracelet held such a store of secret equipment? It was perfect. However, when Emma put on her bracelet, she saw that the lock was loose. Without the bracelet locking properly, all the charms might fall off. That was not good.

"Mom!" yelled Emma.

Her mom rushed in. "Is everything all right? We need to hurry."

"I know," said Emma and then she began to whisper, "but look, the lock on my bracelet is loose. What happens if it falls off when I'm OM?" OM was short for on mission. Emma's mom knew that.

"Keep calm, I think I might have something," whispered Mom. "Come on, let's go to my bedroom."

"Your bedroom?" Then Emma remembered. "Oh, right, got you."

Emma took off her bracelet and put it in her pocket. She then put the book back on the shelf and pressed the button under her desk. As she closed the drawer again, the book locked into the shelf. Emma then followed her mom down the hallway.

They looked back into the kitchen where they could see that Bob had moved on to eating a stack of toast. He wouldn't notice them. They walked on into Emma's parents' bedroom. Mom opened her closet door and pressed a small button on the hinge. The back of the closet slid back revealing a secret room. A room with a desk and a laptop and a wall covered with certificates, lots of certificates—all of them with the **SHINE** logo. It was SJ45's office.

"Okay, let's see," said Mom. She too reached under her desk, opened the second drawer down and went to the bookshelf, opened a book safe and took out a bracelet. "It needs a bit of polish, but otherwise it is in perfect working order. Here." She unlocked the bracelet and slipped her charms off then handed the bracelet to Emma, who then threaded her charms on. Luckily, her mom's bracelet fit her perfectly.

"Well done, Mom, or should I say SJ45."

It was certainly handy having an ex-secret agent for a mom.

# Chapter • 4

Emma would normally report to **SHINEHQ** via the Mission Tube, a secret underground transportation system that took agents to key **SHINE** locations. Each agent had their own access point and the access point for EJ12 was at her school, in the girls' bathroom at her school, to be exact. But today was Sunday and the school was locked. It was exactly for moments like these that **SHINE** had the Light Shop, a small ordinary-looking store on a small, ordinary-looking street. What was less ordinary was that underneath the store, twenty floors down, was

**SHINE HQ**. As her mom drove, Emma switched on the radio just as another news report was beginning.

"Continuing our earlier story about the strange changes to the water in a city reservoir, it seems another reservoir has also been affected. Authorities still have no clues as to what has happened but fear if more reservoirs are shut down, the city's water supply will be in danger."

*Is the mission something to do with this water disappearing?* Emma wondered, as her mom slowed down and stopped the car.

"Okay, sweetie, I mean Agent EJ12, here we are."

"Thanks, Mom," said Emma, opening the door.

"Good luck and don't forget to give the new password to the lady," called her mom, as she pulled out from the curb and drove away.

Emma stood outside the Light Shop. "We shine a light!" said the sign in the window and Emma smiled at that as she pushed the door open. A buzzer went off. She looked around, but no one seemed to be there. Strange. She walked around, ducking under all the lights hanging from the ceiling and then, seemingly from nowhere, an elderly lady appeared.

"Hello," she said. "May I help you?"

"Hello," replied Emma. "I hope so." And then she remembered the new secret password exchange. "I am very interested in lava lamps, do you have any?"

"Oh, yes we do, please follow me," said the woman. She led Emma to the counter at the back of the store. The woman went behind the counter and took out a small black box. "Would you be so kind as to put your hand on here?" said the lady, smiling as she placed the box in front of Emma.

Emma put her hand on the box, which buzzed for a moment then stopped. A small green light on the side of the box glowed.

"How lovely!" said the lady. "You are cleared for access, Agent EJ12. Please take the elevator to level 20 and await further instructions."

EJ went to the elevator and the doors opened. She walked in and looked at the elevator buttons. There were buttons from 0 to 8, but that didn't worry EJ. She simply pressed 2 and 0 and waited as the doors closed. There was a sudden whoosh and EJ's ears popped before the elevator stopped. EJ was at level 20, actually -20 to be precise—she was now twenty floors below ground level.

"Welcome, Agent EJ12," said a digital voice as the doors opened. "Exit elevator and turn left. Continue until you come to the Code Room."

EJ walked until she came to a plain metal door with a small keypad and screen next to it. She keyed in her pin code and another digital voice spoke.

"Security test commencing. State your name."

"Emma Jacks," said EJ in a clear, loud voice.

"State your favorite ice cream flavor."

EJ didn't have to think about that one. "Double chocolate chip with caramel crunch," she said.

"Welcome, EJ12. Door opening."

EJ12 had reached the Code Room.

The Code Room at **SHINE**"s **HQ** was a very small, simple, yellow-painted room with a chair, a table with paper and a pen, and a long, clear tube coming from the ceiling and ending directly over the table. The messages came via the tube and EJ expected a small canister to come whizzing down with a coded message for her to work on. She was, therefore, a little taken aback when a very large canister slowly pushed its way down the tube before being squeezed out onto the table. There was a large label on the outside.

For EJ12's eyes only.
Papers intercepted en route to a
known SHADOW despatch point
08.31. Sent to EJ12 09.17.
Urgent decode required.

EJ took the canister and unscrewed the lid. She pulled out a thick wad of paper stapled three times down the left-hand side. It had a bold heading on the front page and some numbers were scrawled across the top in pen.

*SM2 S4 . 48 - 106 - 111 - 131 - 173 - 179 - 185 - 188*

FOR CAST AND CREW ONLY
SHOOTING SCRIPT
**SPY MOVIE 2**

**SCENE 4**
It is a foggy night. Agent White, in a black trench coat, collar up, is standing under the dim light of a street-lamp. Agent Black, also in a black trench coat, appears from out of the shadows. She approaches the first woman cautiously.

BLACK (whispering)
The first geese fly backward tonight.

WHITE (turning)
No they don't.

BLACK (in whisper)
Don't turn around. It's the password.

WHITE (now also whispering)
Right, I get it, sorry. Start again.

BLACK (sighs)
The geese fly backward tonight.

WHITE (slowly)
I hope they don't hit anything.

BLACK
Agent White confirmed. We are ready to go.
You can't drop the ball on this one.

WHITE
Drop what ball?

BLACK (crossly)
It's an expression.

WHITE (coughs)
I knew that. No sweat.

BLACK
The first stage is complete. But that was only small.
Only the start. Now we move to the next, bigger stage
(then loudly, too loudly) Mwah ha ha!
(coughs, embarrassed, then whispers again) All is ready.

WHITE
But what if they find our stuff? Should we move it?
It will be easy to, it would only take a second.

BLACK
No, location is secure. Stand by.

WHITE
Stripe, I mean check. I'm on my way.
(Agent Black turns but walks into lamppost.)

EJ read the script and read it again, but she couldn't see any code. But there had to be one and she had to find it, fast.

# Chapter • 5

EJ looked again at the handwritten note across the top.

*SM2 S4 . 48 - 106 - 111 - 131 - 173 - 179 - 185 - 188*

*If there is a code here, and there must be,* she thought, *then there has to be a connection between this writing and the script.* EJ knew from her **SHINE** code-cracking training that codes had keys and once you found the key you could unlock the code. Was this handwritten note the key? EJ looked at the first part.

*SM2 S4 .*

*SM2, what is that?* EJ asked herself. It wasn't a code, at least not one EJ recognized, so what was it? Then EJ looked to the top of the page and read SPY MOVIE 2. *Is SM2 simply short for Spy Movie 2? And if it is, what is S4 short for?* EJ read down and saw "scene 4." Was S4 scene 4? "Too easy!" cried EJ out loud.

But then she looked at the next bit of the note and thought perhaps it wasn't so easy. There were no more letters, just numbers. EJ realized that the code had changed.

*These numbers have to stand for something and they have to stand for something to do with the script for scene 4 of* Spy Movie 2, *but what is that? They probably don't stand for letters because none of the numbers are the same.* EJ looked hard at the numbers again.

*48 – 106 – 111 – 131 – 173 – 179 – 185 – 188*

Then she noticed something. The numbers were in order, starting with the smallest number and getting bigger.

*I wonder,* thought EJ. She looked at the script and began counting the words from the start, writing the number above the word. "It" was 1, "is" was 2, "a" was 3, "foggy" was 4 ... EJ kept going, counting off the words. When she got to word 48, she circled the word. If EJ was right, word 48 was the first word of the secret message and that word was "first." EJ wrote it down on a piece of paper.

First

EJ kept on numbering each word and got to the 106th word, circled it and wrote it down next to the first.

First ball

And then she did the same for 111, 131, 173, 179, 185 and 188, writing each word down.

## SCENE 4

1 2 3   4    5    6    7   8 9 10   11    12

It is a foggy night. Agent White, in a black trench coat,

13  14 15  16      17  18  19  20  21 22 23

collar up, is standing under the dim light of a street-

24    25    26    27 28 29 30   31    32    33

lamp. Agent Black, also in a black trench coat, appears

34  35 36 37   38      39    40      41  42

from out of the shadows. She approaches the first

43        44

woman cautiously.

45        46

BLACK (whispering)

47 48  49 50    51        52

The (first) geese fly backward tonight.

53    54

WHITE (turning)

55 56  57

No they don't.

58  59  60

BLACK (in whisper)

61  62    63    64 65    66

Don't turn around. It's the password.

67    68 69    70

WHITE (now also whispering)

71  72 73 74  75    76    77

Right, I get it, sorry. Start again.

*78    79*

BLACK (sighs)

*80  81  82    83        84*

The geese fly backward tonight.

*85      86*

WHITE (slowly)

*87 88  89   90  91   92*

I hope they don't hit anything.

*93*

BLACK

*94    95      96    97 98  99 100 101*

Agent White confirmed. We are ready to go.

*102 103   104 105 106 107 108 109*

You can't drop the (ball) on this one.

*110*

WHITE

*111  112 113*

(Drop) what ball?

*114     115*

BLACK (crossly)

*116 117    118*

It's an expression.

*119    120*

WHITE (coughs)

*121 122   123  124  125*

I knew that. No sweat.

126

BLACK

127 128 129 130 131 132 133 134 135 136

The first stage is complete But that was only small.

137 138 139 140 141 142 143 144 145 146 147

Only the start. Now we move to the next, bigger stage

148 149 150 151 152 153 154

(then loudly, too loudly) Mwah ha ha!

155 156 157 158 159 160 161 162

(coughs, embarrassed, then whispers again) All is ready.

163

WHITE

164 165 166 167 168 169 170 171 172 173 174

But what if they find our stuff? Should we move it?

175 176 177 178 179 180 181 182 183 184 185

It will be easy to it would only take a second

186

BLACK

187 188 189 190 191 192

No, location is secure. Stand by.

193

WHITE

194 195 196 197 198 199 200 201

Stripe, I mean check. I'm on my way.

202 203 204 205 206 207 208

(Agent Black turns but walks into lamppost.)

When she had finished, EJ looked at what she had written.

*first ball drop complete move to second location*
*48 –106 –111 –   131   – 173–179– 185 –    188*

That had to be the secret message. It was clearly an instruction but for what and for whom? And what did it all have to do with *Spy Movie 2?*

EJ needed to get this back to **SHINE** and fast. She rolled the script back up, tucked in the paper with the decoded message and put it all back into the canister and sent the canister back up the message tube. It was sucked away toward the **SHINE** Operations Room where the head of **SHINE**, A1, would be waiting for it.

# Chapter • 6

When EJ12 walked through the two sliding metal doors to enter the **SHINE** Operations Room, she was surprised to find that all the lights were off. Had there been another *SHADOW* attack on the **SHINE** energy plant? But then EJ noticed that the Light Screen was glowing in the center of the room. The Light Screen was like the **SHINE** brain, or at least, how you could see into the **SHINE** brain. You could call up any of the SHINE files, access the Internet, look at photos and maps from the **SHINE** space satellite, track agents, make video calls and, it seemed, watch movies.

As EJ moved farther into the room, she could see that A1 and everyone else in the Operations Room was watching a movie on the Light Screen. She saw some other agents from the under-twelve division. Even from the back, EJ recognized the dark, wavy hair of GP12, one of the fast-transportation agents, along with KM12. EJ always wondered if her name stood for Grand Prix. Next to GP with dark-blond shoulder-length hair was NW11, the current **SHINE** rock climbing champion and next to her, with her shiny straight blond hair, lighter than EJ's, was GH12, trampolining expert. But why were they all watching a film? *Is that appropriate?* wondered EJ. *I mean, it is an awesome screen but shouldn't everyone be working? After all, there has been a mission alert.* Then EJ saw that they were watching *Spy Movie.* Suddenly she heard a familiar voice.

"Light Screen, pause movie, lights up."

The movie stopped and, as the lights went on, a woman with long white hair, curled up into a rather messy bun with two pencils and a pen sticking out, got up and walked toward EJ, smiling broadly. It was A1, the head of **SHINE**.

"Welcome back, EJ12," said A1. "I suppose you thought we were just watching a movie?"

*How does she do that?* wondered EJ. A1 seemed to have this knack of knowing what her agents were thinking, as if she were reading their minds. It was extraordinary, and also, at times, a little embarrassing.

"But, as you can see," continued A1, "we are watching *Spy Movie,* studying it closely to see if we can learn anything. And it is an excellent opportunity for Agents GP12, NW11 and GH12 to develop their clue-finding skills. You know the **SHINE** motto, 'Look for the clue in front of you': connections are often right in front of our eyes."

"Connections between what?" asked EJ.

"We are not completely sure," replied A1, "but we think there is a link between the filming of the new *Spy Movie* and what has happened to the city's water. Through our sources, we have found out that the storyline of *Spy Movie 2* is about an evil agency trying to poison a water supply and now there is the message from a known *SHADOW* agent on the script of *Spy Movie 2.*"

"It does seem too much of a coincidence," agreed EJ, "but what does that message mean?"

"What indeed?" said A1. "We will look at that in a moment, but first I need to show you all something we received a few days ago." A1 turned back to the screen. "Light Screen, show *SHADOW* video message."

"*SHADOW* sent us a video message?" asked EJ, hardly believing her ears. "In code?"

"No, this message they wanted us to understand," said A1, as a grainy image came on screen. "I think you will see why. Light Screen, play video."

The video was very dark; all EJ could make out was a silhouette, a shadowy figure. *I suppose that's appropriate,* EJ thought, smiling.

"Yes, very funny, EJ12," said A1, "but watch closely now."

*Did I say that out loud?* thought EJ, but then she focused as the figure began to talk. Although EJ thought the voice belonged to a woman, it hardly sounded human. *It must have been put through a voice scrambler,* thought EJ.

"Correct," said A1. "The voice has been scrambled. All we can confirm is that it is a female voice."

*This is getting ridiculous,* thought EJ. *And now I have missed the first part of the message.*

"Light Screen, replay video," said A1.

This time EJ tried not to think about anything else as she listened.

"**SHINE**," the voice began, "you have something that belongs to us and we want it back. We want you to hand over Dr. Caterina Hill. If you don't do as we say, you will find things might dry up a bit. We want your answer in twenty-four hours."

And then the screen went black. EJ was stunned. Dr. Caterina Hill was one of *SHADOW*'s cleverest and most evil scientists and she would do anything to make money. She had already tried to melt the polar ice cap and had stolen **SHINE** inventions. But EJ had caught her twice and Dr. Hill was now in **SHINE** detention. It was unthinkable that **SHINE** would give her back so she could start more evil schemes.

"We can't give her back to them, can we?" NW11 asked A1.

"No, of course not, NW," replied A1, "but I am extremely worried about what *SHADOW* will do when we don't. We received this message two days ago. We ignored it. We didn't want *SHADOW* to think they could do what they want, but then this happened." A1 turned to face the screen again. "Light Screen, show eastern reservoir."

Two photos flashed up on the screen. On the left was a reservoir nearly full of water and on the right was a photo of the same area but now looking like a reservoir of pink jelly.

"Is that the reservoir that was on the news?" EJ asked.

"It is," confirmed A1. "The picture on the left is the reservoir last week and the one on the right is the same reservoir today. And look at this, EJ12. Light Screen, zoom right photo."

The photo on the right enlarged and EJ could see that there were hundreds, no thousands, of small pink balls.

"They turned the water pink?" asked EJ. "That's weird but is it bad?"

"Very, but it gets worse," said GH12.

"We then received this second message," said A1. "Light Screen, play second video."

Again, it was the same grainy video, the same shadowy figure and the same robotic voice talking. "You are not as bright as you think, **SHINE**. Did you think we were joking? You did not answer so we left something pink to make you think. If we get Dr. Hill, we will release the antidote. If we do not, the balls will harden and there will be no more water. Ever." The screen went black.

"'Something pink to make you think.' Bad

poetry," said EJ. "It can't be *SHADOW* Agent Adriana because we already have her in **SHINE** detention too."

"Correct again," said A1. "My evil twin sister is also safe under top security. So it seems there is a new scientist at *SHADOW*. Someone we don't know about. And the pink, EJ, the pink in the message has to be the pink balls in the reservoir."

"But what are they?" asked GP12.

"And what do they do?" added EJ. "Have they taken the water?"

"Well, yes and no," said A1. "The pink balls are SAPs, Super-Absorbent Polymers."

"Pardon?" said EJ.

"No, not pardon, polymers. Chemical crystals that are able to absorb or soak up water, enormous amounts of water. They start as tiny balls, but they can absorb up to five hundred times their weight in water."

"They can? Those little balls? How?" asked EJ.

"Let's see," said A1, turning to the Light Screen.

"I think we need a demonstration. Light Screen, video conference Professor H2O. Agents GP12, NW11 and GH12, please move to the surveillance screens and monitor the movie crew movements."

As the other agents headed to their computer consoles, an image of a young woman with curly brown hair appeared on the Light Screen.

"Good morning, A1, Agent EJ12," said Professor H2O.

"Good morning, Professor," replied A1. "Can you please show us what a SAP can do?"

"I would be delighted," said Professor H2O. She took a small jar from her pocket and unscrewed the lid. She then dipped her finger into the jar and pulled it out again, holding her finger close to the camera.

"Can you see these little balls, EJ?"

EJ nodded.

"Watch what happens when I put them into this glass of water."

EJ watched in amazement as the balls became large and jellylike and the water from the glass seemed to disappear.

"That's impossible!" exclaimed EJ. "The water," she cried, "it's gone!"

"No," said H2O, "not gone, absorbed. Isn't it clever? These were first used to keep babies' diapers drier, but now, with drought becoming more and more common, scientists are also finding ways to use them to store water. By using them we can reduce the need for watering dramatically! But now it seems that *SHADOW* has added something to the standard SAP chemical mix, something that absorbs the water but then hardens the balls to keep the water trapped. We are trying to work out what we can add that will release the water."

"The message I decoded talked about a ball drop," said EJ. "Do you think that these are the balls they mean?"

"Yes, EJ12," said A1. "Light Screen, new panel, show decoded message."

A square flashed next to the image of Professor H2O and the message EJ had cracked appeared.

Message intercepted from
SHADOW 08.31.

Sent to EJ12 09.17.

Decoded message returned to
SHINE 09.33.

Time taken to decode 16.00.

FIRST BALL DROP COMPLETE
MOVE TO SECOND LOCATION

"So the ball drop must mean dropping SAP balls
into the water supply," said EJ. "And now they are
planning to drop more balls. But where?"

"We are not sure yet," said A1, turning to the Light
Screen again. "Show city map, highlight reservoirs."

A map flashed on screen with five areas of blue
around the edge of the city. The smallest one was
now flashing pink.

"You see, EJ," continued A1, "the pink spot is
where *SHADOW* has already struck and the blue
areas are the other city reservoirs. Two have been

hard hit by the drought and are nearly empty, but the other two, the two quite close together, are nearly full. We think they will be *SHADOW*'s target. And there's one more thing. Light Screen, show movie crew location."

A red light flashed on the map, right between the two larger reservoirs. The location set of *Spy Movie 2* was right next to the two large reservoirs.

"Too many coincidences," agreed EJ. "So what is the plan?"

"We, or rather you, are going to go undercover. We need to get you on that location shoot to see what you can find out."

"I'm going on a movie set," said EJ, trying not to sound incredibly excited.

"Yes, is that a problem?" asked A1.

"Oh, no," said EJ, smiling. "Not at all."

# Chapter • 7

EJ walked into the **SHINE** dressing room and saw the regulation **SHINE** undercover gear, summer-issue, laid out on a chair: a black T-shirt, black shorts, socks and sneakers. She quickly changed into the clothes, which were, as always, a perfect fit, and came back into the Operations Room and up to A1, who was standing behind a high workbench.

"Right, EJ, we think you might need to add these to your charm bracelet for this mission."

EJ saw four new charms laid out on the bench: a star, a heart, what looked like a little book and a lipstick.

"You want me to wear lipstick?" asked EJ, surprised.

"No, you are much too young!" said A1. "You twist the charm and it transforms into what looks like a normal lipstick but is actually a truth gloss. When it is applied, a chemical is released onto the lips and the person wearing it must tell the truth. Not only that, the person will not remember anything. The truth gloss causes a hypnotic trance."

*Hmmm,* thought EJ, *if I could only get some on Bob, I could find out the truth about my diary … although, how would I get him to put on lipstick?*

"I am sure I don't need to remind you, EJ, that charms are strictly for mission use."

"Of course, A1," replied EJ quickly. *There she goes again!* EJ thought it best to move the conversation on. "And what does the star charm do?"

"This is a star tracker charm," said A1. "You simply put it on something, or someone, and you can follow the star. This charm is one of the few that actually gets smaller when you twist it. It reduces to a tiny spot that no one would ever notice. And, you use it with your phone or this." A1 picked up the little book charm.

"A book?" suggested EJ.

"Close. It is a secret notebook, a spy pad," replied A1.

"Why do I need a spy pad?" said EJ. "I can just use my phone."

"Well yes, you could," agreed A1. "But sometimes a bigger screen can be useful and this spy pad has a few extra apps of its own which we are very excited about. But first we must set up your security code. Please activate your spy pad charm, EJ."

EJ took the charm from the bench and twisted it at the top. Within seconds she was holding an indigo-colored case with the **SHINE** logo on the back. On the front was a series of buttons and small lights and what looked like a speaker in the bottom corner.

"Please state your name and code name into the microphone speaker," instructed A1. "Speak clearly and slowly."

EJ held the book up close and said, "Emma Jacks, Agent EJ12."

One of the lights flashed green and the screen came on. EJ read the next set of instructions.

AGENT IDENTITY CONFIRMED.
VOICE RECOGNITION ACTIVATED.
USE KEYPAD TO KEY IN DAY AND
MONTH OF YOUR BIRTHDAY.

"That will be your password," explained A1. "The voice recognition feature and the code will mean only you will be able to use the book."

*That would save a lot of problems at home,* thought EJ, as she keyed in "99." For a girl who loved math, she had an excellent birthday, the ninth day of the ninth month. Even better, she had been born at nine minutes past nine in the morning. After EJ keyed in the number, a second light flashed and the book opened. Now EJ could see a large screen with small app pictures on it.

"Now touch on the app with an X on it," said A1. "Then hold the spy pad up to the cupboard under the bench."

EJ did and gasped. "That's amazing!" she cried. On the screen she could see what was behind the cupboard door. On the top shelf she could see boxes with the SHINE logo on them and, on the lower shelf, a row of motorbike helmets.

"Indeed," said A1, smiling. "We are rather happy with our new X-ray app. It allows agents to see through walls and doors without drawing attention to themselves. X-ray goggles do tend to be a giveaway. We took the idea from airport scanners. The book also has a camera and photo printing app and ..."

"A1!" Agent GP12 called out suddenly. "We have an update."

"Go ahead."

"Agent CC12 has just called in to advise that *Spy Movie 2* delivery vehicles are in the final stages of packing and preparing to depart."

"Then we need to hurry, EJ," said A1. "You can

familiarize yourself with the rest of your charms later. There are delivery trucks taking equipment to the set of *Spy Movie 2* and you need to get yourself on one of those trucks and onto the movie set. We need to find out if there really is a connection between this movie and *SHADOW*'s plot to destroy the city's water—and do it before they strike again. One more thing, EJ12: no one must know you are there."

"Of course," said EJ.

"Now, please take one of those helmets from the cupboard. Agent KM12 from our fast-transportation division is waiting in the exit tunnel. She will get you to the delivery depot and into the van undetected."

EJ smiled. KM12 was one of her best spy buddies. She hadn't seen her since **SHINE** camp.

EJ left the Operations Room via a door that led to the exit tunnel. In the tunnel was KM12 standing next to a bicycle with a passenger car. There was a sticker on the bike: "Speed of Light Couriers."

EJ ran up to her friend and gave her a hug. "Nice touch with the courier sign, but why can't I just ride on the back?"

"You'll see," said KM, smiling. "Here, put on this leather jacket and your helmet and hop in. We need to move, EJ."

EJ pulled on her gear, climbed into the sidecar and gave KM the thumbs-up. KM turned on the bike and began to peddle. As she did, the bike began to move, but as fast as a motorbike and without a sound: it was a new electric-powered bike, good for the environment and perfect for secret drop-offs. KM steered the bike up the tunnel. They seemed to be approaching a dead end, but she pushed a button on her bike and the wall slid to one side. The two agents rode out into a quiet alley.

"We will be at the drop in twenty minutes, EJ," said KM. "We then need to get you onto one of the movie delivery trucks. Agent CC says that there is a ramp at the back of each truck and I think we can deliver *you* straight into one of those vans."

"But how?" asked EJ.

"Do you see the lever on the front of the side car?" replied KM. EJ nodded. "That will disengage the sidecar from the bike and allow you to steer it. When we approach the van, you need to pull the lever, release the sidecar and steer it up the ramp into the van. Push the lever down to brake and you can then pull the truck door shut and lock it from the inside. Activate Eco-Deco on the sidecar to dispose of it once you are secure within the locked van. Check?"

"Check," said EJ. "This will be fun!"

The two girls smiled at each other as the bike sped along. There were definitely worse things than being part of **SHINE**. It was almost a pity when KM began to slow the bike down.

"Okay, EJ," said KM, "we are approaching the delivery depot. I'll circle around the area once so we can get our bearings."

As KM rode around the fence of the delivery

depot, EJ could see that there was a wide driveway leading up to a warehouse. There were forklifts buzzing around and women loading boxes onto dollies. In front of the warehouse were six large delivery vans all in a row and all with ramps leading up to their backs. There was also a road leading out the back of the depot. EJ scanned the trucks.

"I'm going to come in that back road, EJ," said KM.

"Okay and let's take the last truck," replied EJ. "It's farthest from the warehouse and it looks nearly full. You can ride straight past it and then turn around. I can release the sidecar on the way back."

"Okay, EJ, let's do it," said KM.

KM took the bike up a gear and tore up the back road. She was so fast and so quiet that none of the delivery women noticed them. KM rode past the trucks, then turned around and began to ride back, making sure she stayed in line with the last delivery truck. EJ waited until she could see the inside of the van and then pulled the lever. The sidecar came away from the bike and continued straight at the van. KM peeled off to the right and sped off down the road and out of the depot.

"Good luck, EJ, you will do great!" cried KM. "I'm out of here!"

EJ held the lever tight and kept it straight. As she approached the van, she pushed the lever down to slow the sidecar. She felt a bump as it hit the ramp. The sidecar was in the truck. EJ pushed the lever down hard and stopped just before hitting a pile of boxes. She was in. She leapt out of the car and put her jacket and helmet in the seat before reaching under it. Her fingers felt for the small Eco-Deco button she knew would be there. One push and the sidecar and its contents would disintegrate: it was an excellent, although rather smelly **SHINE** way to dispose of equipment so it wouldn't be found. EJ pinched her nose as the belching noises came from the car and within a minute there was nothing left. EJ ran to the back of the truck and pushed the button on the side wall. The ramp lifted up and locked in place. *Just in time,* thought EJ, as she heard two women's voices coming closer to the truck.

"This one's already locked up and ready to go," said one woman.

"Okay, let's take it," said the other. "We can make the first delivery."

EJ sat still as the women climbed into the front of the truck and started the engine. They didn't know it, but there would be one more thing delivered to the movie set—EJ12.

# Chapter · 8

From the back of the truck, EJ could hear the delivery women talking to each other.

"Can you believe what a drama queen that Sydney Radisson is?" said one. "She went off at the director yesterday, accusing her of ruining the scene, then yelling at the lighting assistants that they had made her look bad. She was horrible! And then she started on the catering supervisor, demanding to know where her special chocolates were. Can you imagine? Fifty double-fudge chocolate bars! Crazy!"

*That doesn't sound so crazy,* thought EJ. *Sounds rather delicious, actually.*

"I know," said the other woman, "and then she accused her personal assistant of spilling her perfume bottles. The poor assistant kept trying to tell her she didn't do it, but Ms. Radisson just kept yelling at her."

EJ blushed a little when she heard that. It sounded a little like the way she had behaved with Bob. Perhaps he really hadn't known that she had a diary?

"And then she started yelling at everyone, telling them that no one must open her bottles. Apparently this precious perfume comes inside little balls and they went everywhere."

*Balls?* thought EJ and she remembered the message she had decoded: "First ball drop a success." *Just another coincidence?* wondered EJ. *I need to see those perfume bottles.*

Then EJ held on to the side of the truck as it turned sharply and onto what felt like a rough dirt track. After a bumpy ten minutes or so, it came to a halt.

"Here we are," declared one of the delivery women, opening the cab door. "Let's get this load unpacked and head back for the next one."

EJ needed to find somewhere to hide. She turned on her phone and used its light to quickly assess her hiding options. There were big boxes everywhere, but all of them were taped shut. Then EJ spied three tall white cubicles on the other side of the boxes. She climbed over to see what they were. There were doors on them and on each door was a sign.

*Prestige*
*Porta Potties*
★
*Posh Portable Toilets*
*for the Stars*

EJ groaned. Somehow all her missions ended up involving a bathroom. There was a loud bang as the truck door began to open. There was no more time. EJ opened a porta potty door and went in. She locked the door behind her, sat on the toilet seat lid and waited. She could hear the women unloading the boxes, the dolly wheels squeaking as they rolled up and down the ramp. Then she heard the sound of heavy boots close to the porta potty.

"Give me a hand, will you?" It was one of the delivery women. "I just need to tilt this one onto the dolly."

EJ stuck both her arms out to the sides of the porta potty and pushed hard against the walls to make sure she didn't fall off the toilet seat as it was tilted on its side and taken off the truck.

"Is it just me or does this one feel heavier?" asked one woman.

EJ held her breath.

"Maybe a bit," replied the other. "Let's put it down here."

EJ breathed a quiet sigh of relief when the dolly stopped and the porta potty was set down. She listened as the sound of the footsteps went away and the truck drove off. Then slowly, quietly, she opened the porta potty door, just a tiny crack so she could see out. She seemed to be in some kind of outdoor delivery area and, as there didn't seem to be anyone around, she slipped out of the porta potty and made her way through the piles of delivery boxes. Now she could hear voices and as she came past the last row of boxes, she walked out on what looked like a huge pop-up, temporary village.

EJ wasn't sure what she was expecting the movie location set to be like, but it wasn't this. She thought there might be a few cameras and a few lights, the actors, obviously, and then a few more people behind the scenes. What she didn't expect to see was this mini city. Everywhere there were trucks, trailers and tents. There were tents with kitchens and tables and chairs, tents with racks of clothes and tents with equipment: lights, cameras, computers and what looked like an endless supply of electric cable. And there were so many people running around, talking frantically into earpieces and phones, carrying clothes, carrying cups of coffee, that EJ couldn't really see what was going on. But as she watched, she saw that all the frantic activity was centered on an area far ahead where equipment and people ringed a clearer spot. Suddenly, a loud voice cut through all the noise.

"Okay everyone, quiet on the set …"

EJ could see a woman holding a megaphone and sitting on a director's chair on the edge of the clear area. There were two women with large cameras on either side of her and three other women with large spotlights. *The woman in the chair must be the director,* thought EJ.

"And, action!" cried the director.

Everything went silent then EJ heard another woman talking.

"You, you, you …"

"And cut," said the director through the megaphone. "Sydney, the line is, 'You won't catch me!' Can you remember that? It's quite a small line."

"Well, like obviously, I was distracted, I ..."

"Okay then, let's go again. Quiet everybody and, action!"

"You won't catch it! Oh, shoot!"

"And cut!" cried the director, her voice sounding tired and more than a little irritated. "Okay, people, let's take five. Sydney, we need to talk about your lines."

Everyone started talking again and EJ watched as the camerawomen moved cameras to new locations, lighting women adjusted lights and other people wrote on clipboards and talked noisily into phones.

"I need to get a bit closer," she said to herself, "and without being noticed." And then she walked into a large box, knocking it over. A few people turned around at the noise, but EJ quickly ducked behind another box.

*Not a great start to not being noticed,* thought EJ, but then as she looked at what fell out of the box, she thought it might have been a clever move after all. EJ had knocked over a box of clothing and she picked up a pink cap with the word CREW across the top.

"Perfect," said EJ, as she put the cap on and walked out of the storage area and toward the set. She clipped her phone to her shorts and put in her earpiece. Next she took her spy pad charm and activated it and put it under her arm. Now with her crew cap, phone and spy pad, she looked busy and involved like everyone else.

As EJ walked on, she could see that the set location was divided into different areas. There was the catering area with huge camping stoves and long tables and benches where people sat having coffee. There was the technical area with film equipment, cameras and large spotlights all stored in large vans. There was a costume department with racks and racks of clothes and boots, including a whole rack of black trench coats just like the one Sydney Radisson wore in *Spy Movie*. It was there that EJ spied a lanyard with a security card hanging on a coat hanger on one of the racks. EJ looked around and then casually picked up the pass. It was a lighting crew pass. Someone must have left it there.

*Lighting, that's appropriate for a* **SHINE** *agent,* thought EJ. She took her spy pad, whispered her code name and keyed in her code. She then pressed the photoshop app and smiled. There was a quick flash, EJ looked at the screen, pressed a few buttons and waited. A green light went on and a small passport-sized photo slid out from a slit at the bottom of the spy pad.

"Not my best, but it will do," said EJ, as she took the photo, peeled off the back and stuck it over the existing photo on the pass. If no one looked too closely, they would never know. Special Agent EJ12 was now officially on location.

# Chapter · 9

EJ left the costume area and headed up toward the clear area and the large circle of people. As she approached, she could see scaffolding nearly thirty feet high with a platform at the top on which four people were standing. As EJ walked around to where she could see the other side of the scaffold, she realized it had been made up to look like the outside of an office building, and the women on top of the platform now looked as if they were standing on the roof of a high-rise office tower. Next to them was another high scaffold, but this one had an elevator and cameras attached so the camerawomen could film at any height. On the ground, in front of the building facade, was a large pile of foam mattresses, like the ones EJ used at gymnastics. As EJ got closer, she could see it was Sydney Radisson on the platform holding a white fluffy cat, surrounded by three other women, one with a can of hairspray and a comb, one with a little case and one holding a bottle of water. Sydney looked bored and cross.

*She looks much smaller, and grumpier, in real life*, thought EJ.

"Okay, let's get ready to go again," cried the director through her megaphone. "We are going to try the jump scene again. This is scene six. Agent White is being chased by Agent Black and is now standing on the top of a building. She calls after her and then jumps, carefully avoiding the four old ladies walking their poodles. Okay, everybody, cue old ladies, cue poodles!"

From the side, four old ladies, wearing long coats and carrying canes walked out, each with a small black poodle on a red leash.

79

"Perfect, old ladies, keep walking, please. Camera one, stay on the ladies, camera two on the poodles, please, and cue Sydney."

Sydney Radisson passed her cat to the woman holding the water bottle and stepped forward to the edge of the platform.

"Perfect and check hair," cried the director.

The girl with the comb rushed forward and fiddled with Sydney's hair before spraying enormous amounts of hairspray over it.

"Thank you," cried the director. "Makeup check, please,"

The other girl came forward and brushed some powder on Sydney's cheeks and applied some lipstick and then stepped back out of the camera shot.

"Okay, lighting is good, roll cameras and action!"

Sydney put her hand up as if to shield her eyes from the sun and looked out and then down toward the ground. She looked behind her and called out, "You won't catch me!" Then she leaned forward over the edge of the platform.

"And cut! At last! Beautiful, Sydney, just beautiful, darling," the director cried. "Cue stunt. Camera three get ready for the jump."

Sydney stood back and snatched her cat back from the assistant while another woman, dressed in exactly the same costume and with identical hair as her stepped forward.

"And action!"

While Sydney sipped on her water and stroked her cat, the stuntwoman walked up to the edge of the platform and jumped out and down onto the safety mattresses below. She got up, brushed some dirt off her pants and walked off.

*Sydney doesn't do the stunts,* realized EJ. *She hardly does anything at all!*

"And cut! Okay, people, that's a wrap for this scene. And listen up, there's a change to the schedule. Sydney, we have deleted the speedboat scene. Our next, and your last scene, will be the bridge scene at the reservoir."

Sydney dropped her water bottle and her cat, which nearly fell off the platform. Sydney didn't notice. "That's not supposed to be until tomorrow," she shouted to the director. "I'm not prepared. I need my rest!"

"You will be fine, Sydney, you will be fantastic!" the director reassured her.

"I will not be fantastic. I will be exhausted. You will have to change the schedule."

"I'm sorry, Sydney, I really am, but I can't do anything about it," the director replied. "The city has really stepped up security around the reservoirs and we only have bridge access this afternoon."

"You, you, you ..." stuttered Sydney, her eyes narrowing. "You can't do this! This is unbelievable! I am going to my trailer! I need to rest!"

*After what?* wondered EJ. *She said one line.*

The platform was lowered and Sydney's cat ran off while Sydney stormed off in the direction of a row of silver trailers that were parked at the back of the shooting area. EJ watched as the movie star began furiously texting on her phone.

*Should I follow her?* wondered EJ.

Piinngg!

It was her phone and a message from **SHINE**.

TEXT RECEIVED BY KNOWN
SHADOW AGENT.
SENT FROM YOUR LOCATION:
BRIDGE SCENE 2DAY.

Someone on the set was sending a message to a *SHADOW* agent. EJ looked around—nearly everyone was using a phone. The message could have been sent by any one of the people on the set. But then she looked at Sydney again, who was now almost running to her trailer. EJ had a hunch—and she had learned to follow her hunches—and that meant following Sydney Radisson.

# Chapter · 10

EJ approached the line of trailers. These were the leading actors' trailers, long silver motor homes that became the stars' homes away from home when they were shooting a film on location. There were four trailers, one very large one and three smaller ones. EJ was guessing that Sydney Radisson's was the very large one. She was careful to keep her cap down and stay well back as she trailed Sydney, who was still texting. Was it Sydney who had sent the message to a *SHADOW* agent? Was she texting another one now? If the answer was yes, did that mean Sydney Radisson worked for *SHADOW*?

Suddenly Sydney swung around and stared directly at EJ who also quickly spun on her heels and began to walk in the opposite direction.

"You!" cried out Sydney.

*Is she talking to me?* wondered EJ. *I really hope she is not talking to me.*

"You in the pink cap!"

*Yes, she is. Have I been found out?*

"You! Come here!" shouted Sydney.

EJ turned around slowly.

"Bring me my cat! She's on the chair over there."

EJ leaned over to pick up the fluffy white cat whose tail was twitching from side to side. As EJ picked her up, she noticed her pink collar and shiny, diamond-studded pendant with a large S on it. As the pendant fell across her hand, EJ felt how heavy it was.

"I'd be cross too if I had that thing around my neck," she whispered to the cat. "Come on, let's take you to your grumpy owner."

EJ walked up to Sydney, keeping her eyes

down. "Here you are, Ms. Radisson," she mumbled, holding out the cat.

Sydney grabbed the cat, turned and walked up to the large trailer, opened the door and slammed it shut behind her. EJ relaxed. She hadn't been found out. It seemed Sydney only wanted her cat—even though she didn't seem that fond of it—and to get to her trailer, quickly.

EJ edged closer to the trailer. When she was about six feet from the door she stopped, took out her spy pad and pressed the X-ray app, holding the spy pad in front of her. While to a passer-by it would look as if EJ was just reading something in her folder, she was actually looking right into Sydney Radisson's trailer. But EJ knew she couldn't just stand out in front of the star's trailer. She moved around to the side where she would not be noticed so easily. The inside of the trailer was like a luxury hotel. There were plush red sofas and a long, shaggy white rug on the floor. There was a glass coffee table that held an enormous vase with dozens of white orchids and a bowl of chocolate bars, double-fudge chocolate, EJ assumed. From the roof hung a glittering chandelier. One wall was covered with mirrors and another with a row of black cupboards with gold handles and locks. EJ watched as Sydney put her phone down on the coffee table, picked up a sheet of paper and sat on the sofa. Eating a chocolate bar and stroking her cat, she studied the sheet intently.

*Perhaps she is just learning her lines for the next scene,* thought EJ.

EJ watched for more than half an hour and nothing happened. Sydney just sat and read, eating chocolate bars and checking her phone now and then. Just as EJ was thinking that maybe Sydney Radisson was just a bad-tempered movie star and not a *SHADOW* agent at all, Sydney did something unusual. She checked her phone and then looked back at the papers and wrote something down. She got up, tickled her cat under its neck and then reached up and opened one of the cupboards above the table. She took out three large, pretty-looking bottles, all with a large letter S on the front. There was a pink, an orange and a blue bottle. EJ watched as Sydney shut the cupboard and then tickled the cat under the neck again.

*She really likes her cat,* thought EJ, even though she thought the cat still looked pretty grumpy. *But what are those bottles? I need a closer look.* She zoomed in with her X-ray. The bottles looked like perfume bottles, but they seemed to have something other than liquid in them. EJ zoomed again. They were, as EJ knew they would be, full of tiny balls.

*These must be the bottles the delivery women were talking about,* thought EJ. She watched as Sydney looked at her sheet of paper and picked up the orange bottle and gave it a shake. *What is she doing?*

Then EJ was distracted as a woman ran up to the trailer. Just in case she was seen, EJ stepped back and began talking into her phone as the woman knocked on Sydney's trailer. With her X-ray app, EJ watched Sydney quickly give her cat yet another scratch under the neck and then open the cupboard and put the bottles away before giving her cat one more tickle. She threw the paper she had written on onto the table then looked toward the door and called out. EJ guessed she was saying "Come in," as the woman then entered the trailer.

*Why would Sydney pet her cat if she is in such a hurry and why would she need to hide the bottles?* wondered EJ. Things were definitely getting more suspicious.

EJ could hear voices in the trailer. She couldn't make out the words, but there was no doubt that Sydney wasn't happy. Her voice was getting louder and louder. "If I have to," she finally yelled at the woman, as the door suddenly burst open and she stomped down the steps in her high heels.

EJ came out from beside the trailer and walked past, scribbling furiously on her spy pad. Sydney didn't even look at her as she and the woman walked off.

EJ knew she couldn't keep following Sydney. Sooner or later she would notice her. From what EJ had seen though, she needed to keep tabs on Ms. Radisson, and she'd thought of a way to do it.

EJ walked toward the shooting area and stopped at the catering tent, taking one of the water bottles out of a large fridge. EJ then took her star charm from her bracelet and twisted. Within seconds it shrank to a tiny, sticky star in EJ's hand. EJ hoped her little plan would work. She took a deep breath and shouted out, "Ms. Radisson! Ms. Radisson!"

Sydney Radisson turned back looking surprised and more than a little cross. "Are you talking to me?" she snapped.

EJ ran up to her. "Yes, sorry for yelling, Ms. Radisson, but you forgot your water."

"I have my water right here, can't you see that?" snapped Sydney, glaring at EJ.

EJ gulped. "No, that water is no good," she said, thinking quickly. "This one has added nutrients. It's been especially ordered for you."

"Oh, well in that case, why didn't you say so? Give it to me!" said Sydney, even more rudely this time. "Come on, I don't have all day!"

EJ leaned forward to pass Sydney the bottle and as she did, she pretended to stumble.

"Hey!" cried Sydney, as EJ grabbed the bottom of her trench coat. "What are you doing, you stupid girl?"

"Oh, gosh, I am so sorry," said EJ, stroking Sydney's trench coat back into place. "Sorry, sorry, Ms. Radisson, I tripped. Here is your water. I'll leave now," said EJ.

"Good idea," said Sydney, turning her back on EJ and walking onto the set.

"Yes it was," said EJ to herself, as she reopened her spy pad and pressed the star tracker app. A map appeared on the screen with a yellow star. When Sydney moved, the star would flash as it moved along the map. A red light indicated EJ's position. EJ had successfully put the homing device on Sydney's trench coat and would now know where she was at all times. That was good, very good. But what she most needed to know now was what those little balls were in the perfume bottles. She headed back toward Sydney Radisson's trailer to find out.

Piinngg!

It was another message from **SHINE**. EJ opened it and read.

TEXT TRACE PLACED ON SYDNEY
RADISSON'S PHONE.
INTERCEPTED 11.30.
SENT TO AGENT EJ12 11.33.
POSSIBLE CODED MESSAGE:
FOLLOW 44 TO THE LETTER
5 21 24 15 42   39 24 8 16 23

EJ checked the time. The text was received only three minutes ago. Was that what Sydney had seen on her phone? Was that what made her get up and go to the cupboard? EJ could see the message was clearly a code and if it was a coded message going to Sydney Radisson, then it was confirmed: Sydney Radisson had to be working with *SHADOW*. She was obviously a better actor than EJ had thought. But what was the code? EJ12 would need to find out—and fast.

# Chapter · 11

EJ looked at the message again.

> FOLLOW 44 TO THE LETTER
> 5 21 24 15 42    39 24 8 16 23

She had seen Sydney pick up the paper as soon as she read the text message and then she had seen her write something down. Was that something to do with what "follow 44 to the letter" meant? EJ wasn't sure, but she knew the only way to find out was to get into that trailer and take a look at what Sydney had been reading. She checked the star tracker. Sydney was still over at the set, but EJ may not have enough time. She ran over to the trailer and pulled on the door handle, but the door was locked. Calmly and quickly, checking that no one was watching, EJ took her key charm and twisted it to convert into a larger universal skeleton key. EJ put the key into the lock and turned it smoothly. She then opened the door and stepped up into the trailer, closing it quickly behind her.

*This really is like a five-star hotel,* thought EJ, feeling the soft plush carpet under her feet and, for some reason, she wondered what the bathroom was like. But now was not the time to explore the trailer, she needed to look at the sheet of paper. The piece of paper that Sydney's cat had just walked across on her way to settle on the pink cushion on the sofa. The paper was dirty—and for a moment, EJ's thoughts flashed back to her diary—but intact. EJ picked it up.

## SPY MOVIE 2

**SCENE 44**
Agent White is alone on the bridge of the large reservoir waving a bottle over the edge. A helicopter is hovering above her. Agent Black leans out of the chopper.

BLACK
It's over, White! It's all over!

WHITE
No, I still have the bottle.

BLACK
You are surrounded. Hand it over!

WHITE
Never. Stand back or I will throw it off the bridge.
(Agent White throws the bottle. Agent Black swoops with the chopper in an attempt to catch the bottle but misses.)
Mwah ha ha ha. You won't catch me either!
(She takes out a remote control and presses a button. Another helicopter sweeps into view and lands on the bridge. White jumps in and flies away.)

It was another part of the *Spy Movie 2* script, scene 44. *This script sounds a lot like what SHADOW is trying to do,* thought EJ. *Does "follow 44" mean follow the script of scene 44? It could, but what does "to the letter" mean? Is it the same code as the last script message?* It was worth a try. EJ counted out the words, but the first set of words made no sense at all.

On hovering another over still

　　EJ tried mixing the words up, but they didn't make sense in any order. *I'm counting words,* thought EJ. *What if I count letters, what if I "follow to the letter," will that work?*

　　EJ enlarged the first sentence and counted the letters.

**SCENE 44**

1 2  3 4 5     6  7  8  9 10 11 12  13 14 15 16 17  18 19  20 21 22
**Agent White is alone on the**

23 24 25 26 27 28  29 30  31 32 33  34 35 36 37 38  39 40 41 42 43 44 45 46 47
**bridge of the large reservoir**

48 49 50 51 52 53 54    55 56 57 58 59 60  61 62 63 64  65 66 67   68 69 70 71
**waving a bottle over the edge.**

　　EJ quickly counted through the numbers for the first set, 5-21-24-15-42. The fifth letter was T. The twenty-first letter was H. The twenty-fourth letter was R. The fifteenth letter was O. The forty-second letter was W.

*T-H-R-O-W* spelled out EJ. *Now this is looking more promising. Let's try the second set, let's see, 39-24-8-16-2-3.* The thirty-ninth letter was O. The twenty-fourth letter was, as last time, R. The eighth letter was A. The sixteenth letter was N. The second letter was G. The third letter was E.

O-R-A-N-G-E.  THROW ORANGE.

Throw Orange. Was that it? Was that the message? Orange what? But then, all of a sudden, EJ got it. Orange Balls! The balls in the bottles, the bottles with the big letter S on them. Why didn't she think of that? "S" must stand for *SHADOW*. The bottles contained the balls that *SHADOW* was using to absorb the water. When Sydney was told she was about to shoot the bridge scene, she had requested instructions and the instructions came in the text, telling her that she needed to throw the orange balls over the bridge into the reservoir. And she would be able to do it because she would be on the bridge filming scene 44. It wouldn't even disrupt filming because no one would ever suspect anything wrong was happening because Sydney would be doing exactly what it said in the script! A spy playing a spy, it was the perfect cover—who would ever suspect it? EJ needed to report to **SHINE**. She took out her phone and texted.

SR IS SHADOW.
WILL THROW ORANGE BALLS.

Within seconds, A1 sent back a text.

GOOD WORK!
BUT DO NOT CONFRONT.
SR MUST FINISH FILM.

*Why?* wondered EJ, but before she could ask there was another text.

IF FILM IS NOT COMPLETED.
SHINE AGENCY MAY BE
DISCOVERED.

*So how do I stop her?* thought EJ. Again, she was just about to text her question when A1 texted back.

YOU WILL FIND A WAY.
SEND SAMPLE OF BALLS VIA
FLASK CHARM.
GOOD LUCK.
SHINE OUT.

*At least getting a sample shouldn't be a problem,* thought EJ. She knew the balls were in the cupboard. She checked the tracker and was relieved to see that Sydney hadn't moved from the set. EJ took a charm from her bracelet that looked like a bottle, twisted it and was soon holding a small glass bottle, a charm that was used for scientific testing. An agent simply put a sample into the bottle and pressed the button on the neck. Microchip technology inside the bottle then tested the composition of the sample and transmitted the data back to the SHINE lab for analysis. The lab would then text the agent their findings. EJ had used it before, on a marine mission, and it was easy. At least it was easy once you had the sample.

When EJ went to open the cupboard she had seen Sydney take the bottles from she hit a problem. The cupboard was locked, but it wasn't a key lock so her universal key wouldn't work. It looked like some kind of card-swipe lock, but Sydney hadn't used a card—or had she? In her mind, EJ replayed what she had watched Sydney do and then remembered that she had stroked her cat under the chin before and after opening the cupboard. EJ looked at the little pendant on the cat's collar, the one that was so heavy.

"I wonder," she said, as she felt around the edge of the pendant. "Hold on, little one, I won't hurt you. I just want to look at your pretty pendant." There was a small clip on the side that EJ pushed up. The back of the pendant flipped out and a small metal card fell out. As EJ took the card and slid the back of the pendant into place again, she noticed the cat's name inscribed on the back.

*That's a funny name,* thought EJ. *Does it mean something important?* She pressed her word app on her spy pad and quickly keyed in the name. She smiled when she saw what appeared on the screen.

## SKYGGE: DANISH FOR SHADOW

"Not you too," she said to the cat. But Skygge just rolled over and went back to sleep.

EJ took the card and swiped it. The lock released and she opened the cupboard door. She took out the three bottles and carefully took a little ball from each, placed them in her test flask and pushed the button. While she was waiting for the results to come back from the **SHINE** lab, EJ checked the star tracker. It had started to flash.

"Uh-oh," she said to Skygge. "It seems that your owner is on the move."

And, from the way the little star was flashing on the tracker, Sydney Radisson was moving quickly. Quickly back in the direction of the trailer—and EJ12.

EJ quickly put the bottles back in the cupboard and locked it. She then gently put the card back in Skygge's pendant, stroking the little cat under her chin, just like Sydney had. Skygge began to purr.

"You're not a very good agent," she said to the cat.

EJ checked the tracker again, but she didn't need to; she could hear footsteps coming closer. It was Sydney. There was no time for EJ to leave the trailer.

*Think fast, EJ,* EJ said to herself, as she heard the trailer door opening. *Think really fast.*

# Chapter • 12

"You again! How did you get in here? What are you doing in my trailer? And what on earth are you doing with my orchids?"

EJ was standing next to the coffee table holding the enormous bunch of orchids in her arms, unfortunately most of them upside down. Water was dripping onto the white carpet.

"I'm, um, ah, I am here to fix your flowers, Ms. Radisson," she said.

"By holding them upside down?"

"Um, yes, well, it is good for the circulation of

nutrients," spluttered EJ. "It is the latest thing in floral care," she continued. "Everyone's doing it in L.A."

"Oh, are they?" asked Sydney, sounding a little more interested. "But there was nothing wrong with my flowers."

"Oh but there was, Ms. Radisson," began EJ. "You need to regularly rotate flowers. You see?" And with that, EJ began spinning the flowers around. As she did, water sprayed all over Sydney.

"Stop! You're drenching me!" said Sydney.

EJ stopped spinning the flowers. It had not been her best idea.

"Well, finish up and scram," said Sydney, as she roughly scratched under Skygge's neck then opened the cupboard. She grabbed the orange bottle and shut the cupboard again. Almost without EJ noticing, she put the card key back in Skygge's collar.

"Make sure you are gone when I come back," Sydney snapped. "I have a helicopter to catch." And with that she swept out of the trailer.

EJ, still with a few bedraggled dripping orchids

in her hands, walked to the door and watched in dismay as Sydney climbed into a helicopter that had been waiting in front of the trailers. As a woman with a walkie-talkie strode past the trailer, EJ called out to her, "Where are they going?"

"The reservoir, for the bridge scene," the woman replied. "The director wants to get there quickly, while the light is still good."

"Oh, right, thanks," said EJ. *Oh no,* she thought to herself, watching the chopper lift high into the sky. She couldn't believe that she had just let Sydney walk out the door with the bottle of balls that she was going to throw into the reservoir. And if Sydney did that, the city's water supply would be in real trouble. How was she going to stop her now?

Piinngg!

It was her phone again. Another message from **SHINE**. EJ looked at the screen and saw that it was the results of the test from the **SHINE** lab. But were they too late?

```
ORANGE BALLS 1000X STRONGER
THAN PINK.
BLUE BALLS REVERSE THE
REACTION.
GOOD WORK, EJI2.
YOU HAVE FOUND THE ANTIDOTE!
```

But EJ didn't feel like she had done good work at all. She hadn't found out Sydney's secret early enough, she had messed up in the trailer and now she had let Sydney go to the reservoir. All those things were adding up to a failed mission, something EJ had never done before. She went back into the trailer and stuffed the rest of the orchids in the vase. As she did, she noticed the heart charm on her bracelet. She twisted it and an inscription appeared on the back of the charm.

*Don't sweat the small stuff.*

*That's what Mom said,* thought EJ. *Now SHINE is saying it as well:* don't worry about silly little things, focus on the important things.

"Pull yourself together, EJ12," she said to herself. "I can do this. I know everything I need to. I know Sydney Radisson is going to throw the orange balls into the reservoir. I know which one she is going to because I can follow her on the tracker and I know that, if I need to, I can stop the reaction happening by throwing the blue balls in. There is just one thing I don't know: how am I going to get to the reservoir?"

And then EJ remembered her BESTies. She opened up the BEST app on her phone and flicked through with her finger until she got to the fastest person she knew. She pressed the call button. It rang only once before it was answered.

"Hey, what do you need, EJ?" It was KM12.

"A lift," replied EJ. "Quite quickly."

"That's what I do," said KM12. "Meet me at the delivery area. I'll be there in no time."

EJ ran to the delivery area where the truck had first dropped her. There was no one around, but there was also no sign of KM12.

"Hey, what are you waiting for?" whispered a voice.

"KM, is that you?" whispered EJ.

"Who else would it be, EJ?"

"But where are you?"

"I'm up here."

EJ looked up to see KM12 hovering above her in what looked like a bike crossed with a helicopter. It was a tandem bike and KM was on the back seat. In the middle of the crossbar between the two seats was an upright pole with helicopter blades at the top. EJ could see the blades spinning around, but they were completely silent.

"It doesn't make any noise?" asked EJ.

"Of course not," replied KM. "What kind of secret agent flies a noisy helicopter? This mini-chopper is super-quiet, super-quick and super-easy to fly. It's just like a riding a bike, just a bit higher up!" KM flew lower. "Jump on, EJ!"

EJ climbed on and held on to the handlebars. As she climbed onto the front seat, she saw a button marked E.

"What does the 'E' stand for, KM?" she asked.

"It's the extender seat. Push the button and your seat can extend out to sixty feet."

"Can it really?" asked EJ. That gave her an idea.

"Okay, where to, EJ?" asked KM.

"Sydney Radisson is flying to the reservoir in a chopper. I put a tracker charm on her so we can follow her," said EJ, turning around and handing over her spy pad to KM, who locked it into her dashboard. "From the direction it is flying in, I think it is heading to the largest reservoir, just north of here. If I'm not mistaken, the chopper will land Sydney Radisson on the bridge that runs across the reservoir and then be used in the last scene. We need to get to the bridge, but make sure that no one sees us."

"I'll do my best," said KM, as she pulled the

# Chapter • 13

EJ and KM flew over the location set, over fields and roads, all the time checking where the other helicopter carrying Sydney Radisson was.

"They will be approaching the reservoir any minute, KM," cried EJ through the wind that blew around them. "Will we catch up?"

"Don't worry, EJ, we will," KM replied. "Look ahead, we're nearly there."

EJ looked straight ahead and saw that they were approaching a ring of hills. As they swooped up to the top of one hill, EJ saw that the hills formed a natural basin, a basin filled with water. It was a giant lake that stretched almost as far as you could see and, between two hills on one side, was a concrete bridge.

"Look, KM, there's the bridge," cried EJ. "And yes, there's Sydney's chopper landing on it. Careful, KM, we mustn't let anyone see us."

"No problem," cried KM. "Hold on, I'll take us around to the other side."

KM veered the mini-chopper sharply and flew near the edge of the reservoir and then down close to the water's surface.

"Perfect, KM!" cried EJ. "Now can you take me under the bridge and hide us next to the bridge pylon?"

"You got it, EJ!" cried KM.

As KM flew under and along the bridge, EJ peered at the star tracker. The yellow flash that was Sydney Radisson had stopped moving. EJ kept watching as the red flash that showed her location came closer and closer to the yellow flash.

"Okay, KM, let's slow down, a little bit more, a

bit more and, there, stop and hover!"

KM pulled the mini-chopper to a halt and the mini-chopper hovered just above the water's surface, obscured by the bridge pylon. The star tracker now showed the yellow flash on top of the red flash. Below the bridge, EJ and KM were directly under Sydney Radisson who was on top of the bridge preparing to do her scene.

For a moment there was silence, then EJ heard the director's voice.

"And, ready people, cue helicopter and, action!"

The director had started to film scene 44. EJ heard the chopper above the bridge and then a woman's voice shouting.

"It's over, White! It's all over!"

"No, I still have the bottle," cried Sydney.

EJ was a little surprised that Sydney got her line right the first time, but, then again, she now knew that Sydney was not who she pretended to be. Maybe she was pretending to be forgetful last time.

"You are surrounded," cried the other actor.

"Hand it over!"

EJ knew this was the moment in the script when Agent White threw the bottle off the bridge.

"Okay, KM," she cried. "When Sydney says her next line, that chopper is going to swoop down just under the bridge and then straight back up again. When I say 'now,' I will press the extender button and shoot out from under the bridge to catch the bottle. I need you to keep the chopper steady and then hit the E button again to bring me back under the bridge. It will need split-second timing."

"You are going to catch the falling bottle? Way to go, EJ12!" said KM.

For a moment there was silence and then Sydney said her line. "Never. Stand back or I will throw it off the bridge."

That was Sydney's cue to throw the bottle. EJ knew it was her cue as well.

"Now, KM, now!" cried EJ.

EJ pressed the button and the seat shot forward. She leaned out and with her arms outstretched, looked up to the bridge. She saw something falling. Keeping her eye on it the whole time, she never noticed another, third helicopter, far on the other side of the reservoir that was filming the long-range shots. Thwack. The bottle hit EJ's hands hard, but she held on. She felt a jolt as KM hit the E button again and she was pulled back under the bridge. It was all over in seconds, but EJ had done it: the reservoir was safe. Then, above her, on the bridge, she heard Sydney Radisson's final line.

"Well, you won't catch me."

"I'm not so sure about that," said EJ, as she watched the helicopter above fly away with Sydney on board. Then EJ spotted the lipstick charm on her bracelet. She knew just how to trap Sydney. "KM, we need to get back to Sydney's trailer before she does. Ms. Radisson has one more scene to play."

"You again!" shrieked Sydney Radisson as she entered her trailer to see EJ sitting on her sofa. "Why are you in my trailer this time?"

"I was told to bring this straight to you, Ms. Radisson," said EJ. "It is a new lipstick that's just been released in New York."

"Well, why didn't you say so, girl," cried Sydney. "Gimme, and try not to fall on me this time."

Sydney didn't notice the little smile on EJ's face as she passed her the lipstick. "Ooo, lovely color," the movie star said, and immediately applied the lipstick to her lips. The moment she did, Sydney seemed to enter a kind of trance.

"What is your name?" asked EJ, wanting to make sure the truth charm was working.

"Madge Black," replied "Sydney."

*Oh, that's a surprise,* thought EJ. *It is certainly working.* "Okay, Madge, tell me, is there anything fake here?"

"My nails."

"Yes," replied EJ, "go on."

"So is my hair and I can't act very well either."

*Tell me something I don't know,* thought EJ. "Why did you join **SHADOW**?"

"They gave me stuff—oh and she said I could have this really cool beauty cream."

"She? Who's she?" EJ realized she now had a chance to find out who was the brains behind this plot.

"Professor Tekcor. She's always talking about space, but she has also invented some seriously cool cream that makes all your wrinkles go away. Something to do with gravity, I think. Anyway, she said I could have some."

"If you agreed to destroy the city's water supply?" asked EJ.

"Whatever," Sydney said. "She said she'd fix it once she got her friend back. Hey, you, what ..."

EJ saw that Sydney's eyes were becoming more focused. The truth charm must be wearing off.

"What are you doing here?" Sydney repeated.

"Nothing, Madge," replied EJ to a startled

"Sydney." But this time it was EJ who slammed the door of the trailer—after all, she did have some experience in door-slamming herself—and then she locked the door from the outside and whistled sharply. The trailer jolted as a delivery truck lurched it forward. But this time it was a new delivery truck, one with a bright-yellow lightbulb painted on the door.

"Take her away, KM12. Now, that's a wrap!"

And with that, KM12 drove away with Sydney Radisson banging on the door.

Which reminded EJ, she needed a special delivery herself. She took out her phone and keyed 4-6-6-3. A voice answered immediately.

"**SHINE** Home Delivery Service—straight to your door, anytime, anywhere. We have your location, EJ12, and we are on our way." EJ looked at her watch. If they were quick, she would make it home for the evening movie on TV.

# Chapter • 14

The sun was beginning to set and EJ was beginning to feel more than a little tired. She smiled as the **SHINE** pickup car pulled up near the storage area. She might have arrived in a delivery truck, but she was going home in the **SHINE** limousine. After all, who would notice it on a movie set? As she opened the door and climbed in, the driver's screen slid back. It was Agent LP30.

"Well done, EJ12. We will have you home in no time. There's a Triple-S in the fridge for you."

EJ didn't need to be told twice: a Triple-S was a **SHINE** Super Sub, a roll that A1 herself had created for feeding agents on the move. It was a long bread roll with a hole cut in the top. Bread was then scooped out and the sub was filled with chicken, carrots, cheese, lettuce and tomato plus her own top secret mayonnaise. Nothing ever fell out of the roll. EJ took the sub out of the fridge and started eating. It was good. The driver's screen slid back again.

"I have A1 on the video phone for you, EJ," said LP30.

"Okay, thanks, LP," said EJ, as she leaned forward and touched the widescreen TV that spanned the back of the driver's seat. A1's face appeared on the screen.

"Hello and well done, EJ12. Not only did you stop Sydney Radisson from destroying the large reservoir, you discovered the antidote, which has allowed us to return the first reservoir to normal."

"And," said EJ, "there is another *SHADOW* scientist, Professor Tekcor."

"Yes, EJ," replied A1. "I want to know more

about her. And we still have Dr. Hill."

"So you didn't give her back?" asked EJ.

"Absolutely not, EJ," replied A1. "Thanks to you, we didn't need to."

The limousine turned into EJ's street as A1 continued.

"You must be nearly home now, EJ12, but good work again. Oh, and EJ?"

"Yes, A1?"

"Keep an eye on that naughty kitten of yours. **SHINE** out."

"What, I mean pardon, A1?" said EJ, but it was too late, A1 had gone.

EJ remembered her diary drama. It didn't seem so important anymore, but all of sudden she remembered Inky taking her ribbon and her muddy little paws ...

The driver's screen slid back again.

"**SHINE** home delivery complete, EJ12. See you soon."

"Thanks, LP30."

EJ walked up to her front door and rang the bell. Her mom opened it, as she knew she would.

"Hi, Em," Emma's mom cried, giving her a little hug, and then a little too loudly, "How was Isi?"

"Fine, Mom," said Emma. "What's been happening here?"

"Just watching a movie," replied Mom. "Do you want to join us? It's only just started."

"Oh no, that's okay," said Emma. "I think I'll just go to bed." She walked down the hallway past the living room where Dad and Bob and Inky and Pip were on the sofa. "Bob," Emma said.

"Hmm?" replied her brother.

"I was wrong about the diary. I'm sorry, that was really dumb."

"Yeah," began Bob, but then obviously thought better of it. "Thanks, Em."

Emma smiled as she walked into her bedroom.

A few months later, Emma was at the movies with her best friends, Hannah, Isi and Elle, at a preview of *Spy Movie 2.* As Sydney Radisson came on the screen, the audience cheered. Everyone except Emma.

"It's funny," said Han to Emma. "She has been really quiet lately. I don't think she has been in another movie since this one, has she?"

Emma shrugged her shoulders. "Not sure, Han," she replied. "Oh look, the movie's starting."

And with that, the girls settled down to watch the movie, popcorn and candy in hand. Every now and then one of them would whisper to Emma, "You don't really do that stuff do you, Em?" and Emma would just smile.

Then Isi leaned in toward her and whispered, "I wish I could come OM one time, Em."

"That would be cool," agreed Emma, who wondered if A1 would think it was a good idea. "But I don't see how. Hey, hold on, Is, here comes the final scene."

The girls watched, entranced. Sydney Radisson stood alone on the bridge as a helicopter hovered above her. She threw an orange bottle over the edge and the camera swept across the reservoir and then under the bridge. Just for a moment there was a glimpse of something and someone shooting out from under the bridge on what looked like a bike seat on a pole. It was a girl, a girl with blondish hair, wearing black shorts and a T-shirt with a pink cap. And she was stretching out, as if she were trying to catch something.

"Hey!" Hannah nudged Elle.

"Hey!" Elle nudged Isi.

"Hey!" Isi nudged Emma. "Isn't that you, Em?"

"Um, well ..." began Emma.

"It so was!" cried Isi, trying to whisper, unsuccessfully. "You're a movie star."

And just for a split second she was, with a little help from EJ12!

# Collect them all!

EJ12 GIRL HERO — HOT & COLD

EJ12 GIRL HERO — JUMP START

EJ12 GIRL HERO — IN THE DARK

EJ12 GIRL HERO — ROCKY ROAD

EJ12 GIRL HERO — CHOC SHOCK

EJ12 GIRL HERO — ON THE BALL

EJ12 GIRL HERO — MAKING WAVES

EJ12 GIRL HERO — DRAMA QUEEN